The Giving Bear

Disney's
Winnie the Pooh First Readers

Pooh Gets Stuck
Bounce, Tigger, Bounce!
Pooh's Pumpkin
Rabbit Gets Lost
Pooh's Honey Tree
Happy Birthday, Eeyore!
Pooh's Best Friend
Tiggers Hate to Lose
The Giving Bear
Pooh's Easter Egg Hunt
Eeyore Finds Friends
Pooh's Hero Party
Pooh's Surprise Basket
Pooh and the Storm That Sparkled

Disney's

A Winnie the Pooh First Reader

The Giving Bear

Isabel Gaines

ILLUSTRATED BY Josie Yee

NEW YORK

The Giving Bear

"Umph!" grunted Piglet

as he knocked on Pooh's door.

He had his wagon with him.

It was loaded with stuff.

"Hello, Piglet," answered Pooh.

"What's in your wagon?"

"Things from my house,"
Piglet said. "I'm giving them
to Christopher Robin."

Just then Tigger bounced up.

"Hello!" he said.

He had his wagon, too.

"Hello, Tigger," said Pooh.
"Are you giving your things
to Christopher Robin, too?"

"Yes," answered Tigger.

"So he can give them

to someone who needs them."

11

"Do you have anything

you don't need anymore,

Pooh?" asked Piglet.

"Let me think," said Pooh,

thinking very hard.

But he couldn't think

of a thing.

Along came Christopher Robin.

"I see Piglet's and Tigger's wagons,"

he said. "Are you going

to add anything, Pooh?"

15

"I don't have anything
to give away,"
Pooh said sadly.
"There must be something,"
said Tigger.

"Let's look in the cupboard,"

suggested Piglet.

Pooh opened the cupboard doors.

"Oh, dear!" said Piglet.

"Zowee!" shouted Tigger.

"Wow!" exclaimed Christopher Robin.

"Twenty honeypots!" they said

at the same time.

"Only ten honeypots

have any honey

in them," Christopher Robin said.

"I keep a large supply
of honeypots at all times,"
said Pooh.

"Why is that, Pooh Bear?"

asked Christopher Robin.

"Just in case," announced Pooh.

"In case of what?" asked Piglet.

He was a little afraid

to hear the answer.

"I might find

some especially

yummy honey," Pooh said.

"I would need plenty of pots

to store it in,

so I would never run out."

"ALL honey tastes
especially yummy to you!"
Christopher Robin
reminded Pooh gently.

"Ten pots are more than enough

to store your yummy honey."

"But what if I had a party?"
asked Pooh.
"Everyone would want
some honey,
so I would need a lot."

"Pooh," Christopher Robin said,

"if you had a party,

you would invite your friends

in the Hundred-Acre Wood."

"Ten honeypots hold
more than enough honey
for us," said Piglet.

"Hmm," said Pooh.

He still wasn't sure

he wanted to give away

his honeypots.

"Think of everyone
who could enjoy some honey
if you shared your honeypots,"
said Christopher Robin.

"Then they would all be

as happy as I am!" agreed Pooh.

Pooh decided to give away

ten of his honeypots.

His heart felt twice its size.

"Silly old bear," said

Christopher Robin.

He helped Pooh load

his honeypots onto his wagon.

Can you match the words with the pictures?

cupboard

honeypot

Piglet

stuff

wagon

Fill in the missing letters.

doo_

_igger

t_ink

ho_ey

f_iends

Join the Pooh Friendship Club!

A wonder-filled year of friendly
activities and interactive fun for your child!

The fun starts with:
- Clubhouse play kit
- Exclusive club T-shirt
- The first issue of "Pooh News"
- Toys, stickers and gifts
  from Pooh

The fun goes on with:
- Quarterly issues of "Pooh News" each
  with special surprises
- Birthday and Friendship Day cards
  from Pooh
- And more!

Join now and also get a colorful, collectible Pooh art print

Yearly membership costs just $25
plus 15 Hunny Pot Points.
(Look for Hunny Pot Points 3
on Pooh products.)

To join, send check or money order and
Hunny Pot Points to:

Pooh Friendship Club
P.O. Box 1723
Minneapolis, MN 55440-1723

Please include the following information:
Parent name, child name, complete address,
phone number, sex (M/F), child's birthday,
and child's T-shirt size (S, M, L)
(CA and MN residents add applicable sales tax.)

Call toll-free for more information
1-888-FRNDCLB

Kit materials not intended for children under 3 years of age. Kit
materials subject to change without notice. Please allow 8-10 weeks for
delivery. Offer expires 6/30/99. Offer good while supplies last. Please do
not send cash. Void where restricted or prohibited by law. Quantities may
be limited. Disney is not liable for correspondence, requests, or orders
delayed, illegible, lost or stolen in the mail. Offer valid in the U.S. and
Canada only. ©Disney. Based on the "Winnie the Pooh" works, copyright
A.A. Milne and E.H. Shepard.

Fun
for kids
ages 3-8!

Pooh
Friendship
Club

Poo

Help your child learn MATH and READING with a computer and a silly old bear.

©Disney

Disney's Learning Series on CD-ROM

...t your child on the path to success in the 100 Acre Wood, ...here Pooh and his friends make learning math and reading ...n. Disney's Ready for Math with Pooh helps kids learn all the ...portant basics, including patterns, sequencing, counting, ...d beginning addition & subtraction. In Disney's Ready to ...ad with Pooh, kids learn all the fundamentals including the ...phabet, phonics, and spelling simple words. Filled with ...gaging activities and rich learning environments, the 100 ...cre Wood is a delightful world for your child to explore ...er and over. Discover the magic of learning with Pooh.

NEW! Disney's Learning Series

Once Again The Magic Of Disney Begins With a Mouse

Wonderfully Whimsical Ways To Bring Winnie The Pooh Into Your Child's Life.

Pooh and the gang help children learn about liking each other for who they are in 5 charming volumes about what it means to be a friend.

These 4 enchanting volumes let you share the original A.A. Milne stories — first shown in theaters — you so fondly remember from your own childhood.

Children can't help but play and pretend with Pooh and his friends in 5 playful volumes that celebrate the joys of being young.

Pooh and his pals help children discover sharing and caring in 5 loving volumes about growing up.

FREE*
Flash Cards Attached!
A Different Set With Each
Pooh Learning Video!

* With purchase, while supplies last.

Printed in U.S.A. © Disney Enterprises, Inc.